DATE DUE

D1269555

Fast Dan

Written by Mary E. Pearson
Illustrated by Eldon C. Doty

Children's Press®
A Division of Scholastic Inc.
New York • Toronto • London • Auckland • Sydney
Mexico City • New Delhi • Hong Kong
Danbury, Connecticut

For M.F.G.—I look forward to many "good-nights"
with you and a good book
—M.E.P.

To Alex, my first grandson
—E.C.D.

Reading Consultants
Linda Cornwell
Literacy Specialist

Katharine A. Kane
Education Consultant
(Retired, San Diego County Office of Education
and San Diego State University)

Library of Congress Cataloging-in-Publication Data
Pearson, Mary (Mary E.)
    Fast Dan / written by Mary E. Pearson ; illustrated by Eldon C. Doty.
    p. cm. — (Rookie reader)
    Summary: Dan does everything quickly, except when it is time to go to bed.
    ISBN 0-516-22239-2 (lib. bdg.)   0-516-27494-5 (pbk.)
    [1. Speed—Fiction. 2. Stories in rhyme.] I. Doty, Eldon, ill. II. Title. III. Series.
PZ8.3.P27472 Fas 2002
[E]—dc21   2001008349

CHILDREN'S PRESS, AND A ROOKIE READER®, and associated logos are trademarks
and or registered trademarks of Grolier Publishing Co., Inc. SCHOLASTIC and
associated logos are trademarks and or registered trademarks of Scholastic Inc.
1 2 3 4 5 6 7 8 9 10 R 11 10 09 08 07 06 05 04 03 02

Dan is fast!
Dan zips by!

He won't go slow.
He won't even try.

He is fast
when he brushes.

He is fast
when he walks.

He is fast
when he reads.

He is fast
when he talks.

"Slow down," says his mother.

"Slow down," says his dad.

"Slow down," says his teacher.
Dan says, "Slow is bad."

He is fast when he writes.
He is fast when he dresses.

16

He is fast when he eats.
He is fast making messes!

"Slow down," says his sister.
"Slow down," says his aunt.

"Slow down," says his team.
Dan says, "I just can't!"

19

He is fast
when he cleans.

He is fast
when he rides.

He is fast when he runs.

He is fast when he slides.

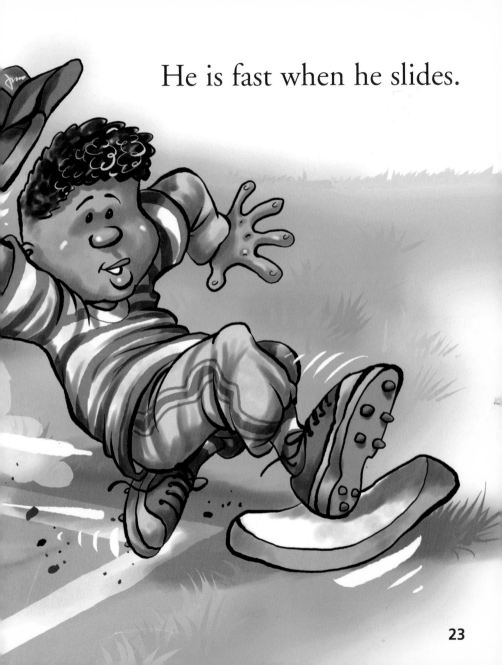

But there is one time
when Dan thinks slow is right—

when he has to go to bed,
when he has to say, "Good night."

"Hurry up," says his mother.
"Hurry up," says his dad.
"Hurry up!" they both tell him.

Dan says, "Fast is bad."

"Good night."

"Good night."

"Good night."

"Good night."

Word List (56 words)

aunt	even	mother	team
bad	fast	night	tell
bed	go	one	there
both	good	reads	they
brushes	has	rides	thinks
but	he	right	time
by	him	runs	to
can't	his	say	try
cleans	hurry	says	up
dad	I	sister	walks
Dan	is	slides	when
down	just	slow	won't
dresses	making	talks	writes
eats	messes	teacher	zips

About the Author

Mary E. Pearson is a writer and teacher in San Diego, California.

About the Illustrator

Eldon Doty is a fifty-eight-year-old illustrator living with his wife and little dog Soupy in Santa Rosa, California. He graduated from the University of Washington and later attended art school at the San Francisco Academy of Art. His favorite activities include traveling, reading history books, riding his motorcycle, and, of course, drawing silly pictures. Many years ago he had a little boy who was like Fast Dan, but he has now grown up to be a policeman.